The Christmas WIND

STEPHANIE SIMPSON McLELLAN

BROOKE KERRIGAN

Red Deer Press

The wind shoved Jo sideways, stealing feeling from her fingers and toes. It chased her with ghostly moans and creepy shrieks. The day before Christmas and still no snow. She should have been glad, but the skinny road seemed colder without it.

Jo hitched her baby brother higher on her hip. Leaving was the right thing to do, but the timing was bad. Her mother's eyes were slippery and her forehead shiny, and Christopher was still so new.

The wind elbowed Jo's mother and kicked her to the ground.

"Stop it!" Jo shook her fist at the sky. Ignoring her, the wind stole her scarf and blew out the light.

Her plan was to be on a bus halfway to someplace else by now, but they weren't even close to the station.

She pulled her mother to her feet. With a howl, the wind forced them off the road and into the prickly fields.

The farm to her left belonged to an old man as unfriendly as the wind.

Franklin Murdock. His very name felt like a curse. The loss of his wife and only baby on a Christmas Eve long ago had turned him so crusty and mean, even grown-ups were afraid of him.

Jo squinted toward Murdock's barn. The old grouch won't be out on a night like this, she thought. Only those who are running from something would brave such a wind.

"Lean on me, Mom. There's a barn across this field. We'll start out again in the morning. Maybe you'll feel better. Maybe the wind will die." But when her mother steadied herself against Jo's shoulder, Jo feared she might drop her brother.

"Okay," she said. "New plan. I'll get Christopher to the barn and come back for you. I'll be fast."

The barn was farther away than it looked.
The more the wind pushed, the more Jo stumbled.
She said words she knew she wasn't allowed to say.
    Reaching the yard, she hid behind a tree. Noting the single light
in the simple house, she darted to the barn, faster than the wind itself.

While it wasn't exactly warm inside, at least the wind couldn't find them in here. She wrapped her coat around her little brother and laid him in an empty manger.

The cattle started lowing softly in the stalls around them. Quiet braying, and the gentle baa of sheep joined in and rose above the stalls in a kind of lullaby. "Quiet yourselves," Jo whispered.

The wind fought her all the way back to her mother. It jostled and bumped them as they limped and stopped and limped their way back to the barn.

As she laid her mother in the
hay, heat rushed to Jo's face.
The manger was empty.

"Where is he?" Jo eyed the cows. She darted from stall to stall and fished frantically through the hay.

But Christopher was gone.

"Franklin Murdock." This time Jo's words were a growl.

Grabbing a shovel, she raged toward the house and peered through the window.

Against the far wall, a wooden trunk spewed blankets and old photographs into the small room. An overturned bottle dripped milk off the edge of the table. The old man sat by the fire with his head in one hand and a crude wooden cradle at his feet.

Jo pushed away from the window.

She charged the front door and banged on it with her fist. The wind held its breath long enough for her to hear movement inside, but the door didn't open.

She hammered louder.

This time Murdock opened the door a crack.

Jo gripped the shovel like a weapon.

"What are you doing with my shovel?" said Murdock.

"You stole our baby. Give him back right now or you'll be sorry."

Murdock frowned and reached for the shovel.

She jerked it out of his reach. "Now!"

"I didn't steal any baby," said Murdock.

"I saw him with my own two eyes."

"That blasted wind carried his wailing right to my door," said Murdock. "I saved him from freezing to death. What was he doing in my barn?"

"None of your business."

"My barn, my business."

"Just give him back," said Jo.

"Where are your parents?" Murdock asked. "Where do you live?"

The wind shifted noisily as Jo looked the old man square in the face. She pressed her lips together and scowled.

"Well, you can't stay in my barn," Murdock said.

"Fine." Jo raised the shovel again. "Just give me my brother and we'll leave your precious barn."

"That's not what I meant." He opened the door wider. "Come inside where it's warm. We'll figure things out in the morning."

Jo eyed him suspiciously. "There's something else you need to know."

Murdock's eyebrows pinched into a single gray line. "And what would that be?"

"My mother is sick." Jo gestured toward the barn with the shovel.

As Murdock leaned out to look, the wind snuck behind him. It shoved him into the yard and blew the barn door open.

Jo raced to keep up. When Murdock knelt beside her mother, muttering gruff words under his breath, she raised the shovel in warning.

"It's the three of us or nothing."

"What are you doing out on a night like this, anyway?" Murdock struggled to his feet with Jo's mother in his arms.

"Just be careful with her," said Jo.

"Tell me your names, at least," said Murdock.

"My mother's name is Merry. I'm Jo."

As they stepped into the rising storm, the wind blew both ways at once and a path of light from a single star opened before them. Jo and Murdock found themselves momentarily suspended between where they came from and where they were going, until an eager blast of air hurried them to the house.

Jo tucked the shovel by the door and
rushed to check on Christopher.

Murdock laid Merry
on the couch by the fire
and fetched some blankets.

"She's had a bad cough for days," said Jo. "Can you phone a doctor?"

"I don't have a phone." Murdock glanced at the old photos still scattered on the floor. "But even if I did, no one will help on Christmas Eve."

He turned his back on Jo and took a seat by the door. With his head in his hands, he stared at the floor.

"What are you doing?" Jo planted herself in front of him. "You can't give up like that."

She swept her arm around the room. "Things won't get better on their own."

Murdock lifted his head. The crumpled lines of his face rearranged themselves.

"Yes ma'am," he said, standing.

The wind prowled in circles around the house as Murdock brought a cool cloth and some medicine for Merry. He warmed some soup for Jo, and laid out some bread and cheese.

Merry tossed in her sleep and whimpered. Christopher cried and then quieted. Together Jo and Murdock kept the two of them comfortable, and the fire blazing.

As the sky deepened from violet to indigo, thousands of stars watched over the house.

"Why don't you rest, Jo?" said Murdock. "I'll stay up and keep watch."

"Wait." Jo put a finger to her lips. "Listen." Murdock looked from the baby to Merry and then back at Jo.

"The wind," she said. "It's stopped."

Silence swaddled the small room. As Jo and Murdock looked out the window, delicate white flakes flew towards them like a host of angels.

Jo yawned.

"You know," she said. "You're not really as horrible as they say."

Murdock snorted. "I guess I could say the same about you."

"Who said I was horrible?" said Jo.

Murdock winked.

He made a nest of blankets by the fire and tucked Jo in. Through heavy lids, she watched him cross the room to the window. With one hand on the sill and the other on his hip, he stood for a long time looking out.

When pale morning light slipped through the window, Jo opened her eyes. A scent, fresh like frost and crisp like fruit, mingled with the comfortable smell of the still crackling fire. Her brother made small sounds as he sucked on his fist. Her mother stirred and sighed. Murdock slouched in a chair, bent sideways in sleep.

So, thought Jo. He didn't keep watch after all.

But then she looked around the room.

Fresh cedar draped the window sills and a Christmas tree leaned in the corner. Threads of straw wove like gold ribbon through the greenery, pinched in places by scraps of colored cloth tied into awkward bows. Silver spoons dangled from the branches, and presents, wrapped in newsprint, crowded beneath.

Kneeling by the tree, Jo touched each package. One was shaped remarkably like the shovel she'd brandished the night before.

"Merry Christmas, Jo," Murdock said from behind her.

"Merry Christmas, Mr. Murdock," she whispered.

Together they opened the door and
marveled at the blanket of snow the
Christmas wind had blown in.

The world that stretched before
them looked fresh and new.

To my Father — *BK*

For Jeff, Sarah, Eryn and Trysten, and dedicated to the 32 schools who participated in *The Christmas Wind Story Project* and the 1,697 students who visualized Jo's determination and Murdock's awakened compassion as they made this story their own. (ChristmasWindStoryProject.com) — *SSM*

J. C. Erhardt Memorial (Makkovik, NL) • Northern Lights Academy (Rigolet, NL) • A.P. Low Primary (Labrador City, NL) • Amos Comenius Memorial (Hopedale, NL) • Holy Family Catholic (Bowmanville, ON) • Northern Lights Public School (Aurora, ON) • St. John The Baptist School (Hamilton, ON) • Monsignor Michael O'Leary School (Bracebridge, ON) • Saint Mary Catholic School (Huntsville, ON) • Mohawk Gardens Public School (Burlington, ON) • St. Thomas Aquinas (Toronto, ON) • Coyote Creek Elementary (Surrey, BC) • Cloverdale Catholic School (Surrey, BC) • Hyland Elementary (Surrey, BC) • Grey Mountain Primary School (Whitehorse, YK) • Mangilaluk School (Tuktoyaktuk, NT) • Sam Pudlat School (Cape Dorset, NU) • Spruceland Traditional Elementary (Prince George, BC) • Warren Peers School (Acadia Valley, AB) • Victoria School (Kamsack, SK) • École Powerview School (Powerview, MB) • Roméo Dallaire Public School (Ajax, ON) • Lennoxville Elementary (Lennoxville, QC) • Centreville Academy (Centreville-Wareham, NL) • Belfast Consolidated School (Pinette, PE) • Forest Ridge Academy (Barrington, NS) • Campobello Island Consolidated School (Wilsons Beach, NB) • Bertha Shaw Public School (Timmins, ON) • Pinecrest Public School (Timmins, ON) • Main River Academy (Pollard's Point, NL) • J.L.R. Bell Public School (Newmarket, ON) • Glendal Primary School (Glen Waverley, Victoria, Australia)

Text copyright © 2017 Stephanie Simpson McLellan
Illustrations copyright © 2017 Brooke Kerrigan
First published in the United States in 2018

Published in Canada by Red Deer Press, 195 Allstate Parkway, Markham, Ontario L3R 4T8
Published in the United States by Red Deer Press, 311 Washington Street, Brighton, Massachusetts 02135

Red Deer Press acknowledges with thanks the Canada Council for the Arts, and the Ontario Arts Council for their support of our publishing program. We acknowledge the financial support of the Government of Canada through the Canada Book Fund (CBF) for our publishing activities.

ONTARIO ARTS COUNCIL
CONSEIL DES ARTS DE L'ONTARIO
an Ontario government agency
un organisme du gouvernement de l'Ontario

Canada Council   Conseil des arts
for the Arts   du Canada

Library and Archives Canada Cataloguing in Publication
McLellan, Stephanie Simpson, author
The Christmas Wind / Stephanie Simpson McLellan ; illustrated by Brooke Kerrigan.
ISBN 978-0-88995-534-9 (hardback)
I. Kerrigan, Brooke, illustrator II. Title.
PS8575.L457C47 2017   jC813'.6   C2017-901147-X

Publisher Cataloging-in-Publication Data (U.S)
Names: McLellan, Stephanie Simpson, author. | Kerrigan, Brooke, illustrator.
Title: The Christmas Wind / Stephanie Simpson McLellan ; illustrator, Brooke Kerrigan.
Description: Markham, Ontario : Red Deer Press, 2017. |Summary: "On Christmas Eve, a homeless single mother, her daughter and baby seek refuge in a barn, where they are befriended by the curmudgeonly widowed farmer. Together they embrace the spirit of the holidays where a future of peace and happiness may await as the star filled night turns to snow and a white Christmas" – Provided by publisher.
Identifiers: ISBN 978-0-88995-534-9 (hardcover)
Subjects: LCSH: Christmas stories. | Homeless families – Juvenile fiction. | Single parents – Juvenile fiction. | BISAC: JUVENILE FICTION / Holidays & Celebrations / Christmas & Advent.
Classification: LCC PZ7.M354Chr |DDC [Fic] – dc23

Edited for the Press by Peter Carver
Text design, and cover illustration by Brooke Kerrigan
Printed in China by Sheck Wah Tong Printing Press Ltd.